HORRiD HENRY'S
Sizzling Summer

Francesca Simon
Illustrated by Tony Ross

Orion
Children's Books

ORION CHILDREN'S BOOKS
This collection first published in Great Britain in 2016 by
Hodder and Stoughton

1 3 5 7 9 10 8 6 4 2

A CIP catalogue record for this book
is available from the British Library.

ISBN 978 1 5101 0171 5

Printed and bound in Great Britain by Clays Ltd, St Ives plc

The paper and board used in this book are from
well-managed forests and other responsible sources.

Orion Children's Books
An imprint of
Hachette Children's Group
Part of Hodder and Stoughton
Carmelite House
50 Victoria Embankment
London EC4Y 0DZ

An Hachette UK Company
www.hachette.co.uk
www.hachettechildrens.co.uk

CONTENTS

HORRID HENRY'S OLYMPICS

Chomp chomp chomp chomp . . .
Burp.

Ahhh! Horrid Henry scoffed the last
crumb of Super Spicy Hedgehog crisps
and burped again. So yummy. Wow.
He'd eaten the entire pack in seventeen
seconds. No one could guzzle crisps
faster than Horrid Henry, especially
when he was having to gobble them
secretly in class. He'd never been
caught, not even—

A dark, icy shadow fell across him.

'Are you eating in class, Henry?' hissed Miss Battle-Axe.

'No,' said Henry.

Tee hee. Thanks to his super-speedy jaws, he'd *already* swallowed the evidence.

'Then where did this crisp packet come from?' said Miss Battle-Axe, pointing to the plastic bag on the floor.

Henry shrugged.

'Bert! Is this yours?'

'I dunno,' said Beefy Bert.

'There is *no* eating in class,' said Miss Battle-Axe. Why did she have to say the same things over and over? One day the Queen would discover that she, Boudicca Battle-Axe, was her long-lost daughter and sweep her off to the palace, where she would live a life of pampered luxury. But until then—

'Now, as I was saying, before I was so rudely interrupted,' she glared at Horrid

2

Henry, 'our school will be having its
very own Olympics. We'll be running
and jumping and swimming and—'

'Eating!' yelled Horrid Henry.

'Quiet, Henry,' snapped Miss Battle-
Axe. 'I want all of you to practise hard,
both in school and out, to show—'

Horrid Henry stopped listening. It
was so unfair. Wasn't it bad enough

that every morning he had to heave his heavy bones out of bed to go to school, without wasting any of his precious TV-watching time running and jumping and swimming? He was a terrible runner. He was a pathetic jumper. He was a hopeless swimmer – though he did have his five-metre badge . . . Besides, Aerobic Al was sure to win every medal. In fact they should just give them all to him now and save everyone else a load of bother.

Shame, thought Horrid Henry, that the things he was so good at never got prizes. If there was a medal for who could watch TV the longest, or who could eat the most sweets, or who was quickest out of the classroom door when the home bell rang, well, he'd be covered in gold from head to toe.

★

'Go on, Susan! Jump higher.'

'I'm jumping as high as I can,' said
Sour Susan.

'That's not high,' said Moody
Margaret. 'A tortoise could jump higher
than you.'

'Then get a tortoise,' snapped Susan
sourly.

'You're just a lazy lump.'

'You're just a moody meanie.'

'Lump.'

'Meanie.'

'LUMP!'

'MEANIE!'

Slap!

Slap!

'Whatcha doin'?' asked Horrid Henry, leaning over the garden wall.

'Go away, Henry,' said Margaret.

'Yeah, Henry,' said Susan.

'I can stand in my own garden if I want to,' said Henry.

'Just ignore him,' said Margaret.

'We're practising for the school Olympics,' said Susan.

Horrid Henry snorted.

'I don't see *you* practising,' said Margaret.

'That's 'cause I'm doing my *own* Olympics, frog-face,' said Henry.

His jaw dropped. YES! YES! A thousand times yes! Why hadn't he thought of this before? Of course he should set up his own Olympics. And

6

have the competitions
he'd always wanted
to have. A name-
calling competition!
A chocolate-eating
competition! A crisp-
eating competition! A
who-could-watch-the-
most-TVs-at-the-same-

time-competition! He'd make sure he
had competitions that *he* could win.

The Henry Olympics. The
Holympics. And the prizes
would be . . . the prizes
would be . . . masses and
masses of chocolate!

'Can Ted and Gordon and
I be in your Olympics?' said
Perfect Peter.

'NO!' said Henry. Who'd
want some nappy babies

7

competing? They'd spoil everything,
they'd—

Wait a minute . . .

'Of course you can, Peter,' said Henry
smoothly. 'That will be one pound each.'

'Why?' said Ted.

'To pay for the super fantastic
prizes, of course,' said Henry. 'Each
champion will win a massive prize of . . .
chocolate!'

Peter's face fell.

'Oh,' he said.

'And a medal,' added Henry quickly.

'Oh,' said Peter, beaming.

'How massive?' said Margaret.

'Armfuls and armfuls,' said Horrid
Henry. His mouth watered just thinking
about it.

'Hmmm,' said Margaret. 'Well, I
think there should be a speed haircutting
competition. And dancing.'

'Dancing?' said Henry. Well, why not? He was a brilliant dancer. His elephant stomp would win any competition hands down. 'Okay.'

Margaret and Susan plonked down one pound each.

'By the way, that's *ballroom* dancing,' said Margaret.

'No way,' said Henry.

'No ballroom dancing, then we won't enter,' said Margaret. 'And Linda and

Gurinder and Kate and Fiona and
Soraya won't either.'

Horrid Henry considered. He was sure
to win everything else, so why not let
her have a tiny victory? And the more
people who entered, the more chocolate
for him!

'Okay,' said Henry.

'Bet you're scared I'll win everything,'
said Margaret.

'Am not.'

'Are too.'

'I can eat more sweets than you any day.'

'Ha!' said Margaret. 'I'd like to see
you try.'

'The Purple Hand Gang can beat the
Secret Club *and* the Best Boys Club, no
sweat,' said Horrid Henry. 'Bring it on.'

★

THE REAL OLYMPICS ARE HERE!

TIRED OF BORING OLD SWIMMING
AND RUNNING? OF COURSE YOU ARE!

NOW'S YOUR CHANCE TO COMPETE IN THE

HOLYMPICS

THE GREATEST OLYMPICS OF ALL!!!
SPEED-EATING SWEETS! TV WATCHING!
CRISP EATING! BURP TO THE BEAT!

BALLROOM DANCING. SPEED HAIRCUTTING.

Entry Fee £1 for the chance
to win loads of chocolate!!!!!

'Hang on,' said Margaret. 'What's with calling this the Holympics? It should be the Molympics. I came up with the haircutting and dancing competitions.'

''Cause Molympics is a terrible name,' said Henry.

11

'So's Holympics,' said Margaret.

'Actually,' said Peter, 'I think it should be called the Polympics.'

'Shut up, worm,' said Henry.

'Yeah, worm,' said Margaret.

★

'Mum!' screamed Henry. 'MUM!!!!!!!!'

Mum came running out of the shower.

'What is it, Henry?' she said, dripping water all over the floor. 'Are you all right?'

'I need sweets,' he said.

'You got me out of the shower because you need sweets?' she repeated.

'I need to practise for the sweet speed-eating competition,' said Henry. 'For my Olympics.'

'Absolutely not,' said Mum.

Horrid Henry was outraged.

'How am I supposed to win if I can't practise?' he howled. 'You're always telling me to practise stuff. And now when I want to you won't let me.'

★

Bookings for Henry's Olympics were brisk. Everyone in Henry's class – and a few from Peter's – wanted to compete. Horrid Henry gazed happily at the £45 pounds' worth of chocolate and crisps piled high on his bed. Wow. Wow. Mega mega wow. Boxes and boxes

and boxes filled with yummy, yummy
sweets! Giant bar after giant bar of
chocolate. His Holympics would have
the best prizes ever. And he, Henry,
fully expected to win most of them.
He'd win enough chocolate to last
him a lifetime AND have the glory of
coming first, for once.

Horrid Henry gazed at the chocolate
prize mountain.

The chocolate prize mountain gazed
back at him, and winked.

Wait.

He, Henry, was doing ALL the work.
Surely it was only fair if he got *something*
for his valuable time. He should have
kept a bit of money back to cover his
expenses.

Horrid Henry removed a giant
chocolate bar from the pile.

After all, I do need to practise for the

speed-eating contest, he thought, tearing off the wrapper and shoving a massive piece into his mouth. And then another. Oh boy, was that chocolate yummy. In a few seconds, it was gone.

Yeah! Horrid Henry, chocolate-eating champion of the universe!

You know, thought Henry, gazing at the chocolate mound teetering precariously on his bed, I think I bought *too* many prizes. And I *do* need to practise for my event . . .

★

What a great day, thought Horrid Henry happily.

15

He'd won the sweet speed-eating competition (though Greedy Graham had come a close second), the crisp-eating contest AND the name-calling one. (Peter had run off screaming when Henry called him Wibble Wobble Pants, Nappy Noodle, and Odiferous.)

Rude Ralph won 'Burp to the Beat'. Margaret and Susan won best ballroom dancers. Vain Violet was the surprise winner of the speed haircutting competition. Weepy William . . . well, his hair would grow back – eventually.

Best of all, Aerobic Al didn't win a thing.

The winners gathered round to collect their prizes.

'Where's my chocolate, Henry?' said Moody Margaret.

'And there had better be loads like you promised,' said Vain Violet.

Horrid Henry reached into the big prize bag.

Now, where was the ballroom dancing prize?

He pulled out a Choco Bloco. Yikes, was that all the chocolate he had left? He rummaged around some more.

'A Choco Bloco?' said Margaret slowly. 'A *single* Choco Bloco?'

'They're very yummy,' said Henry.

'And mine?' said Violet.

'And mine?' said Ralph.

'And mine for coming second?' said Graham.

'You're meant to share it!' screamed Horrid Henry, as he turned and ran.

Wow, thought Horrid Henry, as he fled down the road, Rude Ralph, Moody Margaret, Sour Susan, Vain Violet, and Greedy Graham chasing after him, I'm pretty fast when I need to be. Maybe I *should* enter the school Olympics after all.

Henry's Holiday Howlers

Who on the beach has the biggest sunhat?

The person with the biggest head.

Where do elephants go on holiday?

Tuscany.

What's grey, has four legs and a trunk?

A mouse going on holiday.

Why didn't Beefy Bert enjoy his water-skiing holiday?

He couldn't find a sloping lake.

HORRID HENRY'S HOLIDAY

Horrid Henry hated holidays.

Henry's idea of a super holiday was sitting on the sofa eating crisps and watching TV.

Unfortunately, his parents had other plans.

Once they took him to see some castles. But there were no castles. There were only piles of stones and broken walls. 'Never again,' said Henry.

The next year he had to go to a lot

of museums. 'Never again,' said Mum
and Dad.

Last year they went to the seaside.

'The sun is too hot,' Henry whined.

'The water is too cold,' Henry
whinged.

'The food is yucky,' Henry grumbled.

'The bed is lumpy,' Henry moaned.

This year they decided to try something different.

'We're going camping in France,' said Henry's parents.

'Hurray!' said Henry.

'You're happy, Henry?' said Mum. Henry had never been happy about any holiday plans before.

'Oh yes,' said Henry. Finally, finally, they were doing something good.

Henry knew all about camping from Moody Margaret. Margaret had been camping with her family. They had stayed in a big tent with comfy beds, a fridge, a cooker, a loo, a shower, a heated swimming pool, a disco and a great big giant TV with fifty-seven channels.

'Oh boy!' said Horrid Henry.

'Bonjour!' said Perfect Peter.

★

The great day arrived at last. Horrid Henry, Perfect Peter, Mum and Dad boarded the ferry for France.

Peter

Henry and Peter
had never been on a
boat before.

Henry jumped on
and off the seats.

Peter did a lovely
drawing.

The boat went
up and down and
up and down.

Henry ran back and forth between the
aisles.

Peter pasted stickers in his notebook.

The boat went up and down and up and down.

Henry sat on a revolving chair and spun round.

Peter played with his puppets.

The boat went up and down and up and down.

Then Henry and Peter ate a big greasy lunch of sausages and chips in the café.

The boat
went up and
down and
up and down
and up and
down.

Henry began
to feel queasy.

Peter began to
feel queasy.

Henry's face
went green.

Peter's face went
green.

'I think I am going to be sick,' said
Henry, and threw up all over Mum.

'I think I'm going to be –' said
Peter, and threw up all over Dad.

'Oh no,' said Mum.

'Never mind,' said Dad. 'I just know
this will be our best holiday ever.'

Finally, the boat arrived in France.

After driving and driving and driving they reached the campsite.

It was even better than Henry's dreams. The tents were as big as houses. Henry heard the happy sound of TVs blaring, music playing, and children splashing and shrieking. The sun shone. The sky was blue.

'Wow, this looks great,' said Henry.

But the car drove on.

'Stop!' said Henry. 'You've gone too far.'

'We're not staying in that awful place,' said Dad.

They drove on.

'Here's our campsite,' said Dad. 'A *real* campsite!'

Henry stared at the bare, rocky ground under the cloudy grey sky.

There were three small tents flapping

in the wind. There was a single tap.
There were a few trees. There was
nothing else.

'It's wonderful!' said Mum.

'It's wonderful!' said Peter.

'But where's the TV?' said Henry.

'No TV here, thank goodness. We've
got books,' said Mum.

'But where are the beds?' said Henry.

'No beds here, thank goodness,' said

Dad. 'We've got sleeping bags.'

'But where's the pool?' said Henry.

'No pool. *We'll* swim in the river,' said Dad.

'Where's the toilet?' said Peter.

Dad pointed at a distant cubicle.

Three people stood waiting.

'All the way over there?' said Peter.

'I'm not complaining,' he added quickly.

Mum and Dad unpacked the car. Henry stood and scowled.

'Who wants to help put up the tent?' asked Mum.

'I do!' said Dad.

'I do!' said Peter.

Henry was horrified. 'We have to put up our own tent?'

'Of course,' said Mum.

'I don't like it here,' said Henry. 'I want to go camping in the other place.'

'That's not camping,' said Dad. 'Those tents have beds in them. And loos. And showers. And fridges. And cookers, and TVs. Horrible.' Dad shuddered.

'Horrible,' said Peter.

'And we have such a lovely snug tent here,' said Mum. 'Nothing modern – just wooden pegs and poles.'

'Well, I want to stay there,' said Henry.

'We're staying here,' said Dad.

'NO!' screamed Henry.

'YES!' screamed Dad.

I am sorry to say that Henry then had the longest, loudest, noisiest, shrillest, most horrible tantrum you can imagine.

Did you think that a horrid boy like Henry would like nothing better than sleeping on a hard rocky ground in a soggy sleeping bag without a pillow?

You thought wrong.

Henry liked comfy beds.

Henry liked crisp sheets.

Henry liked hot baths.

Henry liked microwave dinners, TV, and noise.

34

He did
not like cold
showers, fresh
air, and quiet.

Far off in the
distance the
sweet sound
of loud music
drifted towards
them.

'Aren't you
glad we're not
staying in that awful, noisy place?' said
Dad.

'Oh yes,' said Mum.

'Oh yes,' said Perfect Peter.

Henry pretended he was a bulldozer
that had come to knock down tents and
squash campers.

'Henry, don't barge the tent!' yelled
Dad.

Henry pretended he was a hungry Tyrannosaurus Rex.

'OW!' shrieked Peter.

'Henry, don't be horrid!' said Mum.

Mum looked up at the dark, cloudy sky.

'It's going to rain,' said Mum.

'Don't worry,' said Dad. 'It never rains when I'm camping.'

'The boys and I will go and collect some more firewood,' said Mum.

'I'm not moving,' said Horrid Henry.

While Dad made a campfire, Henry played his stereo as loud as he could, stomping in time to the terrible music of the Killer Boy Rats.

'Henry, turn that noise down this minute,' said Dad.

Henry pretended not to hear.

'HENRY!' yelled Dad. 'TURN THAT DOWN!'

Henry turned the volume down the teeniest tiniest fraction.

The terrible sounds of the Killer Boy Rats continued to boom over the quiet campsite.

Campers emerged from their tents and shook their fists. Dad switched off Henry's CD player.

'Anything wrong, Dad?' asked Henry, in his sweetest voice.

'No,' said Dad.

Mum and Peter returned carrying armfuls of firewood.

It started to drizzle.

'This is fun,' said Mum, slapping a mosquito.

'Isn't it?' said Dad. He was heating up some tins of baked beans.

The drizzle turned into a downpour.

The wind blew.

39

The campfire hissed, and went out.
'Never mind,' said Dad brightly.
'We'll eat our baked beans cold.'

★

Mum was snoring.
Dad was snoring.
Peter was snoring.
Henry tossed and turned. But whichever way he turned in his damp sleeping bag, he seemed to be lying on sharp, pointy stones.

40

Above him, mosquitoes whined.

I'll never get to sleep, he thought, kicking Peter.

How am I going to bear this for fourteen days?

★

Around four o'clock on Day Five the family huddled inside the cold, damp, smelly tent listening to the howling wind and the pouring rain.

'Time for a walk!' said Dad.

'Great idea!' said Mum, sneezing. 'I'll get the boots.'

'Great idea!' said Peter, sneezing. 'I'll get the macs.'

'But it's pouring outside,' said Henry.

'So?' said Dad. 'What better time to go for a walk?'

'I'm not coming,' said Horrid Henry.

'I am,' said Perfect Peter. 'I don't mind the rain.'

Dad poked his head outside the tent.

'The rain has stopped,' he said. 'I'll remake the fire.'

'I'm not coming,' said Henry.

'We need more firewood,' said Dad. 'Henry can stay here and collect some. And make sure it's dry.'

Henry poked his head outside the tent. The rain had stopped, but the sky was still cloudy. The fire spat.

I won't go, thought Henry. The forest will be muddy and wet.

He looked round to see if there was any wood closer to home.

That was when he saw the thick, dry, wooden pegs holding up all the tents.

Henry looked to the left. Henry looked to the right.

No one was around.

If I just take a few pegs from each tent, he thought, they'll never be missed.

When Mum and Dad came back they were delighted.

'What a lovely roaring fire,' said Mum.

'Clever you to find some dry wood,' said Dad.

★

The wind blew.

Henry dreamed he was floating in a cold river, floating, floating, floating.

He woke up. He shook his head. He *was* floating. The tent was filled with cold, muddy water.

Then the tent collapsed on top of them.

Henry, Peter, Mum and Dad stood outside in the rain and stared at the river of water gushing through their collapsed tent.

All round them soaking wet campers were staring at their collapsed tents.

Peter sneezed.

Mum sneezed.

Dad sneezed.

Henry coughed, choked, spluttered and sneezed.

'I don't understand it,' said Dad. 'This tent *never* collapses.'

'What are we going to do?' said Mum.
'I know,' said Henry. 'I've got a very
good idea.'

★

Two hours later Mum, Dad, Henry and
Peter were sitting on a sofa-bed inside a
tent as big as a house, eating crisps and
watching TV.

The sun was shining. The sky was
blue.

'Now this is what I call a holiday!' said
Henry.

Henry's Holiday Howlers

Why did the crab
go to jail?

He kept pinching
things.

What makes the
Tower of Pisa lean?

It doesn't eat much.

What stays in one corner, but
can go all around the world?

A postage stamp.

What do witches use
in the summer?

49   Suntan potion.

HORRID HENRY'S CAR JOURNEY

'Henry! We're waiting!'

'Henry! Get down here!'

'Henry! I'm warning you!'

Horrid Henry sat on his bed and scowled. His mean, horrible parents could warn him all they liked. He wasn't moving.

'Henry! We're going to be late,' yelled Mum.

'Good!' shouted Henry.

'Henry! This is your final warning,' yelled Dad.

'I don't want to go to Polly's!'
screamed Henry. 'I want to go to
Ralph's birthday party.'

Mum stomped upstairs.

'Well you can't,' said Mum. 'You're
coming to the christening, and that's
that.'

'NO!' screeched Henry. 'I hate Polly,
I hate babies, and I hate you!'

Henry had been a page boy at the
wedding of his cousin, Prissy Polly,
when she'd married Pimply Paul.
Now they had a prissy, pimply baby,
Vomiting Vera.

Henry had met Vera once before.

She'd thrown up all over him. Henry had hoped never to see her again until she was grown up and behind bars, but no such luck. He had to go and watch her be dunked in a vat of water, on the same day that Ralph was having a birthday party at Goo-Shooter World. Henry had been longing for ages to go to Goo-Shooter World. Today was his chance. His only chance. But no. Everything was ruined.

Perfect Peter poked his head round the door.

'*I'm* all ready, Mum,' said Perfect Peter. His shoes were polished, his teeth were brushed, and his hair neatly combed.

'I know how annoying it is to be kept waiting when you're in a rush.'

'Thank you, darling Peter,' said Mum. 'At least one of my children knows how to behave.'

Horrid Henry roared and attacked. He was a swooping vulture digging his claws into a dead mouse.

'AAAAAAAAAEEEEE!' squealed Peter.

'Stop being horrid, Henry!' said Mum.

'No one told me it was today!' screeched Henry.

'Yes we did,' said Mum. 'But you weren't paying attention.'

'As usual,' said Dad.

'*I* knew we were going,' said Peter.

'I DON'T WANT TO GO TO POLLY'S!' screamed Henry. 'I want to go to Ralph's!'

'Get in the car – NOW!' said Dad.

'Or no TV for a year!' said Mum.

Eeek! Horrid Henry stopped wailing. No TV for a year. Anything was better than that.

Grimly, he stomped down the stairs and out the front door. They wanted him in the car. They'd have him in the car.

'Don't slam the door,' said Mum.

SLAM!

Horrid Henry pushed Peter away from the car door and scrambled for the right-hand side behind the driver. Perfect Peter grabbed his legs and tried to climb over him.

Victory! Henry got there first.

Henry liked sitting on the right-hand side so he could watch the speedometer.

Peter liked sitting on the right-hand side so he could watch the speedometer.

'Mum,' said Peter. 'It's my turn to sit on the right!'

'No it isn't,' said Henry. 'It's mine.'

'Mine!'

'Mine!'

'We haven't even left and already you're fighting?' said Dad.

'You'll take turns,' said Mum. 'You can swap after we stop.'

Vroom. Vroom.

Dad started the car.

The doors locked.

Horrid Henry was trapped.

But wait. Was there a glimmer of hope? Was there a teeny tiny chance? What was it Mum always said when he and Peter were squabbling in the car? 'If you don't stop fighting I'm going to turn around and go home!' And wasn't home just exactly where he wanted to be? All he had to do was to do what he did best.

'Could I have a story CD please?' said Perfect Peter.

'No! I want a music CD,' said Horrid Henry.

'I want 'Mouse Goes to Town',' said Peter.

'I want 'Driller Cannibals' Greatest Hits',' said Henry.

'Story!'

'Music!'

'Story!'

'Music!'

SMACK!

SMACK!

'Waaaaaa!'

'Stop it, Henry,' said Mum.

'Tell Peter to leave me alone!'
screamed Henry.

'Tell Henry to leave me alone!'
screamed Peter.

'Leave each other alone,' said Mum.

Horrid Henry glared at Perfect Peter.

Perfect Peter glared at Horrid Henry.

Horrid Henry stretched. Slowly,
steadily, centimetre by centimetre, he
spread out into Peter's area.

'Henry's on my side!'

'No I'm not!'

'Henry, leave Peter alone,' said Dad. 'I mean it.'

'I'm not doing anything,' said Henry. 'Are we there yet?'

'No,' said Dad.

Thirty seconds passed.

'Are we there yet?' said Horrid Henry.

'No!' said Mum.

'Are we there yet?' said Horrid Henry.

'NO!' screamed Mum and Dad.

'We only left ten minutes ago,' said Dad.

Ten minutes! Horrid Henry felt as if they'd been travelling for hours.

'Are we a quarter of the way there yet?'

'NO!'

'Are we halfway there yet?'

'NO!!'

'How much longer until we're halfway there?'

'Stop it, Henry!' screamed Mum.

'You're driving me crazy!' screamed Dad. 'Now be quiet and leave us alone.'

Henry sighed. Boy, was this boring. Why didn't they have a decent car, with built-in video games, movies, and jacuzzi? That's just what he'd have, when he was king.

Softly, he started to hum under his breath.

'Henry's humming!'

'Stop being horrid, Henry!'

'I'm not doing anything,' protested Henry. He lifted his foot.

'MUM!' squealed Peter. 'Henry's kicking me.'

'Are you kicking him, Henry?'

'Not yet,' muttered Henry. Then he screamed.

'Mum! Peter's looking out of my window!'

'Dad! Henry's looking out of my window.'

'Peter breathed on me.'

'Henry's breathing loud on purpose.'

'Henry's staring at me.'

'Peter's on my side!'

'Tell him to stop!' screamed Henry and Peter.

Mum's face was red.

Dad's face was red.

'That's it!' screamed Dad.

'I can't take this anymore!' screamed Mum.

Yes! thought Henry. We're going to turn back!

But instead of turning round, the car screeched to a halt at the motorway services.

'We're going to take a break,' said Mum. She looked exhausted.

'Who needs a wee?' said Dad. He looked even worse.

'Me,' said Peter.

'Henry?'

'No,' said Henry. He wasn't a baby.

He knew when he needed a wee and he didn't need one now.

'This is our only stop, Henry,' said Mum. 'I think you should go.'

'NO!' screamed Henry. Several people looked up. 'I'll wait in the car.'

Mum and Dad were too tired to argue. They disappeared into the services with Peter.

Rats. Despite his best efforts, it looked like Mum and Dad were going to carry on. Well, if he couldn't make them turn back, maybe he could delay them? Somehow? Suddenly Henry had a wonderful, spectacular idea. It couldn't be easier, and it was guaranteed to work. He'd miss the christening!

Mum, Dad, and Peter got back in the car. Mum drove off.

'I need a wee,' said Henry.

'Not now, Henry.'

'I NEED A WEE!' screamed Henry. 'NOW!'

Mum headed back to the services.

Dad and Henry went to the toilets.

'I'll wait for you outside,' said Dad. 'Hurry up or we'll be late.'

Late! What a lovely word.

Henry went into the toilet and locked the door. Then he waited. And waited. And waited.

Finally, he heard Dad's grumpy voice.

'Henry? Have you fallen in?'

Henry rattled the door.

'I'm locked in,' said Henry. 'The door's stuck. I can't get out.'

'Try, Henry,' pleaded Dad.

'I have,' said Henry. 'I guess they'll have to break the door down.'

That should take a few hours. He settled himself on the toilet seat and got out a comic.

'Or you could just crawl underneath the partition into the next stall,' said Dad.

Aaargghh. Henry could have burst into tears. Wasn't it just his rotten luck to try to get locked in a toilet which had gaps on the sides? Henry didn't much fancy wriggling round on the cold floor. Sighing, he gave the stall door a tug and opened it.

★

Horrid Henry sat in silence for the rest of the trip. He was so depressed he didn't even protest when Peter demanded his turn on the right. Plus, he felt car sick.

Henry rolled down his window.
'Mum!' said Peter. 'I'm cold.'

Dad turned the heat on.

'Having the heat on makes me feel sick,' said Henry.

'I'm going to be sick!' whimpered Peter.

'I'm going to be sick,' whined Henry.

'But we're almost there,' screeched Mum. 'Can't you hold on until – '

Bleeeechh.

Peter threw up all over Mum.

Bleeeechh. Henry threw up all over Dad.

The car pulled into the driveway.

Mum and Dad staggered out of the car to Polly's front door.

'We survived,' said Mum, mopping her dress.

'Thank God that's over,' said Dad, mopping his shirt.

Horrid Henry scuffed his feet sadly behind them. Despite all his hard work,

 he'd lost the battle. While Rude Ralph and Dizzy Dave and Jolly Josh were dashing about spraying each other with green goo later this afternoon he'd be stuck at a boring party with lots of grown-ups yak yak yaking. Oh misery!

Ding dong.

The door opened. It was Prissy Polly. She was in her bathrobe and slippers. She carried a stinky, smelly, wailing

baby over her shoulder. Pimply Paul followed. He was wearing a filthy T-shirt with sick down the front.

'Eeeek,' squeaked Polly.

Mum tried to look as if she had not been through hell and barely lived to tell the tale.

'We're here!' said Mum brightly. 'How's the lovely baby?'

'Too prissy,' said Polly.

'Too pimply,' said Paul.

Polly and Paul looked at Mum and

69

Dad.

'What are you doing here?' said Polly finally.

'We're here for the christening,' said Mum.

'Vera's christening?' said Polly.

'It's next weekend,' said Paul.

Mum looked like she wanted to sag to the floor.

Dad looked like he wanted to sag beside her.

'We've come on the wrong day?' whispered Mum.

'You mean, we have to go and come back?' whispered Dad.

'Yes,' said Polly.

'Oh no,' said Mum.

'Oh no,' said Dad.

'Bleeeach,' vomited Vera.

'Eeeek!' wailed Polly. 'Gotta go.'

She slammed the door.

'You mean, we can go home?' said
Henry. 'Now?'

'Yes,' whispered Mum.

'Whoopee!' screamed Henry. 'Hang
on, Ralph, here I come!'

Henry's Holiday Howlers

Why did the monkey lie on the sunbed?

To get an orangu-tan.

What do you say to someone who's climbed to the top of the mountain?

Hi!

Why does a seagull live near the sea?

If it lived near the bay, it'd be a bagel.

72

*Doctor, Doctor,
I keep thinking I'm an alien.*

Nonsense, you just need a holiday.

*You're right – I've heard Mars is nice
this time of year.*

What do you call a
boy with a spade
on his head?

Doug.

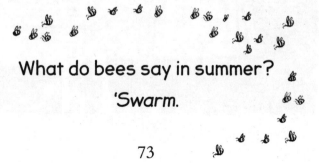

What do you call a
boy without a spade
on his head?

Douglas.

What do secret agents
play on holiday?

I spy.

What do bees say in summer?

'Swarm.

HORRID HENRY MINDS HIS MANNERS

'Henry and Peter! You've got mail!' said Mum.

Henry and Peter thundered down the stairs. Horrid Henry snatched his letter and tore open the green envelope. The foul stink of mouldy socks wafted out.

Yo Henry!

Marvin the Maniac here. You sound just like the kind of crazy guy we want on Gross-Out! Be at TV Centre next Saturday at 9.00 a.m. and gross us out! It's a live broadcast, so anything can happen!

Marvin

'I've been invited to be a contestant on *Gross-Out*!' screamed Henry, dancing up and down the stairs. It was a dream come true. 'I'll be shooting it out with Tank Thomas and Tapioca Tina while eating as much ice cream as I can!'

'Absolutely not!' said Mum. 'You will not go on that disgusting show!'

'Agreed,' said Dad. 'That show is revolting.'

'It's meant to be revolting!' said Horrid Henry. 'That's the point.'

'N-O spells no,' said Mum.

76

'You're the meanest, most horrible parents in the whole world,' screamed Henry. 'I hate you!' He threw himself on the sofa and wailed. 'I WANT TO BE ON *GROSS-OUT*! I WANT TO BE ON *GROSS-OUT*!'

Perfect Peter opened his letter. The sweet smell of lavender wafted out.

Dear Peter,

What a wonderful letter you wrote on the importance of perfect manners! As a reward I would like to invite you to be my special guest on the live broadcast of *Manners With Maggie* next Saturday *at TV Centre at 9:00 a.m.*

You will be showing the girls and boys at home how to fold a hankie perfectly, how to hold a knife and fork elegantly, and how to eat spaghetti beautifully with a fork and spoon.

I am very much looking forward to meeting you and to enjoying your lovely manners in person.

Sincerely,

Maggie.

'I've been invited to appear on *Manners With Maggie!*' said Peter, beaming.

'That's wonderful, Peter!' said Mum. She hugged him.

'I'm so proud of you,' said Dad. He hugged him.

Horrid Henry stopped screaming.

'That's not fair!' said Henry. 'If Peter can be on his favourite TV show why can't I be on mine?'

Mum and Dad looked at each other.

'I suppose he does have a point,' said Dad. He sighed.

'And we don't have to tell anyone he's on,' said Mum. She sighed.

'All right, Henry. You can be a contestant.'

'YIPPEE!' squealed Henry, stomping on the sofa and doing his victory jig. 'I'm going to be a star! *Gross-Out* here I come!'

★

The great day arrived at last. Horrid Henry had been practising so hard with his Goo-Shooter he could hit Perfect Peter's nose at thirty paces. He'd also been practising shovelling ice cream into his mouth as fast as he could, until Mum caught him.

Perfect Peter had been practising so hard folding his hankie that he could do it with one hand. And no one could twirl spaghetti with a spoon as beautifully or hold a knife and fork as elegantly as Perfect Peter.

At nine a.m. sharp, Mum, Henry, and Peter walked into TV Centre. Henry was starving. He'd skipped breakfast, to have more room for all the ice cream he'd be gobbling.

Horrid Henry wore old jeans and dirty trainers. Perfect Peter wore a jacket and tie.

A woman with red hair and freckles rushed up to them with a clipboard.

'Hi, I'm Super Sally. Welcome to TV Centre. I'm sorry boys, we'll have to dash, we're running late. Come with me to the guests' waiting room. You're both on in five minutes.'

'Can't I stay with them?' said Mum.

'Parents to remain downstairs in the parents' room,' said Super Sally sternly. 'You can watch on the monitors there.'

'Good luck, boys,' said Mum, waving.

Sally stared at Peter as they hurried down the hall.

'Aren't you worried about getting those smart clothes dirty?' said Sally.

Peter looked shocked.

'I *never* get my clothes dirty,' he said.

'There's always a first time,' chortled Sally. 'Here's the waiting room. Studios one and two where you'll be filming are through those doors at the end.'

In the room was a sofa and two tables. One, marked *Gross-Out*, was groaning with sweets, crisps and fizzy drinks.

The second, labelled *Manners with Maggie*, was laid with a crisp white cloth. A few dainty vegetables were displayed on a china plate.

Horrid Henry suddenly felt nervous. Today was his day to be a TV star! Had he practised enough? And he was so hungry! His stomach tightened.

'I need a wee,' said Horrid Henry.

'Toilets next door,' said Super Sally.

'Be quick. You're on in one minute.'

Perfect Peter didn't feel in the least nervous. Practice made perfect, and he knew he was. What disgusting food, he thought, wandering over to the *Gross-Out* table.

A man wearing combat fatigues dashed into the room.

'Ah, there you are!' he boomed. 'Come along! It's your big moment!'

'I'm ready,' said Peter, waving his handkerchief.

The man pushed him through the door marked Stage 1.

Henry returned.

A lady in high heels and a pearl necklace poked her head round the door.

'You're on, dear!' said the lady. 'Goodness, you look a little untidy. Never mind, can't be helped.' And she ushered Henry through the door marked Stage 2.

Henry found himself on a brightly lit stage. He blinked in the brilliant lights.

'Let's give a warm welcome to today's guest!' cried a voice. A *female* voice.

The studio audience exploded into applause.

Henry froze. Who was that woman?
Where was Marvin the Maniac?

Something's wrong, he thought. This
was not the set of *Gross-Out*. It was a
pink and yellow kitchen. Yet it looked
vaguely familiar . . .

Meanwhile, on Stage 1, Perfect Peter
shrank back in horror as two gigantic
children carrying Goo-Shooters and
massive bowls of ice cream advanced

towards him. A presenter, laughing like a hyena, egged them on.

'You're not Maggie!' said Peter. 'And I don't know how to use a –'

'Get him guys!' squealed Marvin the Maniac.

'HELLLLP!' shrieked Peter.

SPLAT!

★

Back on Stage 2, Henry suddenly realized where he was.

'Now don't be shy, darling!' said the presenter, walking quickly to Henry and taking him firmly by the hand. 'Peter's here to show us how to fold a hankie and how to eat beautifully!' It was Maggie. *From Manners with Maggie.*

What could Henry do? He was on live TV! There were the cameras zooming in on him. If he screamed

there'd been a terrible mistake that
would ruin the show. And hadn't he
heard that the show must go on? Even
a dreadful show like *Manners with
Maggie*?

Henry strolled onto centre stage,
smiling and bowing.

'Now Peter will show us the perfect
way to fold a hankie.'

Horrid Henry felt a sneeze coming.

'AAAACHOOO!' he sneezed. Then
he wiped his nose on his sleeve.

87

The audience giggled. Maggie looked stunned.

'The . . . hankie,' she prompted.

'Oh yeah,' said Henry, feeling in his pockets. He removed a few crumpled wads of ancient tissue.

'Here, use mine,' said Maggie smoothly.

Henry took the beautifully embroidered square of silky cloth and scrunched it into a ball. Then he stuffed it into his pocket.

'Nothing to it,' said Henry. 'Scrunch and stuff. But why bother with a hankie when a sleeve works so much better?'

Maggie gulped. 'Very funny, Peter dear! We know he's only joking, don't we, children! Now we'll show the girls and boys –'

But Horrid Henry had noticed the table, set with a chocolate cake and a large bowl of spaghetti. Yummy! And Henry hadn't eaten anything for ages.

'Hey, that cake looks great!' interrupted Henry. He dashed to the table, dug out a nice big hunk and shoved it in his mouth.

'Stop eating!' hissed Maggie.
'We haven't finished the hankie
demonstration yet!'

But Henry didn't stop.

'Yummy,' he said, licking his fingers.

Maggie looked like she was going to
faint.

'Show the girls and boys how to use
a knife and fork elegantly, Peter,' she
said, with gritted teeth.

'Nah, a knife and fork slows you
down too much. I always eat with my
fingers. See?'

Horrid Henry waved his chocolate-
covered hands.

'I'm sure it was just the excitement
of being on TV that made you forget
to offer me a slice of cake,' prompted
Maggie. She gazed in horror at the
cake, now with a gaping hole on the
side.

'But I want to eat it all myself!' said Horrid Henry. 'I'm starving! Get your own cake.'

'Now I'm going to teach you the proper way to eat spaghetti,' said Maggie stiffly, pretending she hadn't heard. 'Which we should have done first, of course, as we do not eat dessert before the main course.'

'I do!' said Henry.

'Hold your spoon in your left hand, fork in your right, pick up a teensy tiny amount of spaghetti and twirl twirl twirl. Let's see if my little helper can do it. I'm sure he's been practising at home.'

''Course,' lied Henry. How hard could it be to twirl spaghetti? Henry picked up his spoon, plunged his fork into an enormous pile of spaghetti and started to twirl. The spaghetti flew

round the kitchen. A few strands landed
on Maggie's head.

'Whoops,' said Henry. 'I'll try again.'
Before Maggie could stop him he'd
seized another huge forkful.

'It keeps falling off,' said Henry.
'Listen, kids, use your fingers – it's

faster.' Then Henry scooped a handful of spaghetti and crammed it into his mouth.

'It's good,' mumbled Henry, chewing loudly with his mouth open.

'Stop! Stop!' said Maggie. Her voice rose to a polite scream.

'What's wrong?' said Henry, trailing great strings of spaghetti out of his mouth.

Suddenly Henry heard a high-pitched howl. Then Perfect Peter burst onto the set, covered in green goo, followed by whooping children waving Goo-Shooters.

'Maggie! Save me!' shrieked Peter, dropping his shooter and hurling himself into her arms. 'They're trying to make me eat between meals!'

'Get away from me, you horrible child!' screamed Maggie.

It was the Goo-Shooter gang at last! Better late than never, thought Henry.

'Yeee haaa!' Henry snatched Peter's Goo-Shooter, jumped onto the table and sprayed Tapioca Tina, Tank Thomas and most of the audience. Gleefully, they returned fire. Henry took a step back, and stepped into the spaghetti.

SPLAT!

'Help!' screamed Maggie, green goo
and spaghetti dripping from her face.

'Help!' screamed Peter, green goo
and spaghetti dripping from his hair.

'CUT!' shouted the director.

★

Horrid Henry was lying on the comfy
black chair flicking channels. Sadly,
Manners with Maggie was no longer on
TV since Maggie had been dragged
screaming off the set. *Mischief with
Mildred* would be on soon. Henry
thought he'd give it a try.

Henry's Holiday Howlers

DAD: I hate to say this, but your swimming costume is very tight.

MUM: Wear your own then.

Where did Moody Margaret go on holiday this year?

Alaska.

No, don't worry, I'll ask her.

How is the sea held in place?

It's tied.

MAN: I'd like a return ticket, please.

CLERK: Certainly, sir. Where to?

MAN: Back here, of course.

DAD: Did you enjoy your trip to the seaside?

HENRY: No – a crab bit my toe!

DAD: Which one?

HENRY: I don't know, all crabs look the same to me!

What's the coldest country in the world?

Chile.

Why aren't elephants allowed on the beach?

In case their trunks fall down.

Where do zombies go on holiday?

The Deaditerranean.

HORRID HENRY'S RAID

'You're such a pig, Susan!'

'No I'm not! You're the pig!'

'You are!' squealed Moody Margaret.

'You are!' squealed Sour Susan.

'Oink!'

'Oink!'

All was not well at Moody Margaret's Secret Club.

Sour Susan and Moody Margaret glared at each other inside the Secret Club tent. Moody Margaret waved the empty biscuit tin in Susan's sour face.

'*Someone* ate all the biscuits,' said
Moody Margaret. 'And it wasn't me.'

'Well, it wasn't me,' said Susan.

'Liar!'

'Liar!'

Margaret stuck out her tongue at
Susan.

Susan stuck out her tongue at
Margaret.

Margaret yanked Susan's hair.

'Oww! You horrible meanie!' shrieked
Susan. 'I hate you.'

She yanked Margaret's hair.

'OWWW!' screeched Moody
Margaret. 'How dare you?'

They scowled at each other.

'Wait a minute,' said Margaret. 'You don't think — '

★

Not a million miles away, sitting on a throne inside the Purple Hand fort hidden behind prickly branches, Horrid Henry wiped a few biscuit crumbs from his mouth and burped. Um boy, nothing beat the taste of an arch-enemy's biscuits.

The branches parted.

'Password!' hissed Horrid Henry.

'Smelly toads.'

'Enter,' said Henry.

The sentry entered and gave the secret handshake.

'Henry, why – ' began Perfect Peter.

'Call me by my title, Worm!'

'Sorry, Henry – I mean Lord High Excellent Majesty of the Purple Hand.'

'That's better,' said Henry. He waved his hand and pointed at the ground. 'Be seated, Worm.'

'Why am I Worm and you're Lord High Excellent Majesty?'

'Because I'm the Leader,' said Henry.

'I want a better title,' said Peter.

'All right,' said the Lord High Excellent Majesty, 'you can be Lord Worm.'

Peter considered.

'What about Lord High Worm?'

'OK,' said Henry. Then he froze.

'Worm! Footsteps!'

Perfect Peter peeked through the leaves.

'Enemies approaching!' he warned.

Pounding feet paused outside the entrance.

'Password!' said Horrid Henry.

'Dog poo breath,' said Margaret, bursting in. Sour Susan followed.

'That's not the password,' said Henry.

'You can't come in,' squeaked the sentry, a little late.

'You've been stealing the Secret Club biscuits,' said Moody Margaret.

'Yeah, Henry,' said Susan.

Horrid Henry stretched and yawned.

'Prove it.'

Moody Margaret pointed to all the crumbs lying on the dirt floor.

'Where did all these crumbs come from, then?'

'Biscuits,' said Henry.

'So you admit it!' shrieked Margaret.

 'Purple Hand biscuits,' said Henry. He pointed to the Purple Hand skull and crossbones biscuit tin.

'Liar, liar, pants on fire,' said Margaret.

Horrid Henry fell to the floor and started rolling around.

'Ooh, ooh, my pants are on fire, I'm burning, call the fire brigade!' shouted Henry.

Perfect Peter dashed off.

'Mum!' he hollered. 'Henry's pants are on fire!'

Margaret and Susan made a hasty retreat.

Horrid Henry stopped rolling and howled with laughter.

'Ha ha ha ha ha – the Purple Hand rules!' he cackled.

'We'll get you for this, Henry,' said Margaret.

'Yeah, yeah,' said Henry.

★

'You didn't really steal their biscuits, did you Henry?' asked Lord High Worm the following day.

'As if,' said Horrid Henry. 'Now get

back to your guard duty. Our enemies may be planning a revenge attack.'

'Why do I always have to be the guard?' said Peter. 'It's not fair.'

'Whose club is this?' said Henry fiercely.

Peter's lip began to tremble.

'Yours,' muttered Peter.

'So if you want to stay as a temporary member, you have to do what I say,' said Henry.

'OK,' said Peter.

'And remember, one day, if you're very good, you'll be promoted from junior sentry to chief sentry,' said Henry.

'Ooh,' said Peter, brightening.

Business settled, Horrid Henry reached for the biscuit tin. He'd saved five yummy chocolate fudge chewies for today.

Henry picked up the tin and stopped.

Why wasn't it rattling? He shook it.

Silence.

Horrid Henry ripped off the lid and shrieked.

The Purple Hand biscuit tin was empty. Except for one thing. A dagger drawn on a piece of paper. The dastardly mark of Margaret's Secret Club! Well, he'd show them who ruled.

'Worm!' he shrieked. 'Get in here!'

Peter entered.

'We've been raided!' screamed Henry. 'You're fired!'

'Waaaah!' wailed Peter.

★

'Good work, Susan,' said the Leader of the Secret Club, her face covered in chocolate.

'I don't see why you got three biscuits and I only got two when I was the one who sneaked in and stole them,' said Susan sourly.

'Tribute to your Leader,' said Moody Margaret.

'I still don't think it's fair,' muttered Susan.

'Tough,' said Margaret. 'Now let's hear your spy report.'

'NAH NAH NE NAH NAH!' screeched a voice from outside.

Susan and Margaret dashed out of the Secret Club tent. They were too late. There was Henry, prancing off, waving the Secret Club banner he'd stolen.

'Give that back, Henry!' screamed Margaret.

'Make me!' said Henry.
Susan chased him. Henry darted.
Margaret chased him. Henry dodged.
'Come and get me!' taunted Henry.

'All right,' said Margaret. She walked
towards him, then suddenly jumped
over the wall into Henry's garden and
ran to the Purple Hand fort.

'Hey, get away from there!' shouted Henry, chasing after her. Where was that useless sentry when you needed him?

Margaret nabbed Henry's skull and crossbones flag, and darted off.

The two Leaders faced each other.

'Gimme my flag!' ordered Henry.

'Gimme my flag!' ordered Margaret.

'You first,' said Henry.

'You first,' said Margaret.

Neither moved.

'OK, at the count of three we'll throw them to each other,' said Margaret. One, two, three – throw!'

Margaret held on to Henry's flag.

Henry held on to Margaret's flag.

Several moments passed.

'Cheater,' said Margaret.

'Cheater,' said Henry.

'I don't know about you, but I have important spying work to get on with,' said Margaret.

'So?' said Henry. 'Get on with it. No one's stopping you.'

'Drop my flag, Henry,' said Margaret.

'No,' said Henry.

'Fine,' said Margaret. 'Susan! Bring me the scissors.'

Susan ran off.

'Peter!' shouted Henry. 'Worm! Lord
Worm! Lord High Worm!'

Peter stuck his head out of the upstairs
window.

'Peter! Fetch the scissors! Quick!'
ordered Henry.

'No,' said Peter. 'You fired me,
remember?' And he slammed the
window shut.

'You're dead, Peter,' shouted Henry.

Sour Susan came back with the scissors
and gave them to Margaret. Margaret
held the scissors to Henry's flag. Henry
didn't budge. She wouldn't dare –

Snip!

Aaargh! Moody Margaret cut off a corner of Henry's flag. She held the scissors poised to make another cut.

Horrid Henry had spent hours painting his beautiful flag. He knew when he was beat.

'Stop!' shrieked Henry.

He dropped Margaret's flag. Margaret dropped his flag. Slowly, they inched towards each other, then dashed to grab their own flag.

'Truce?' said Moody Margaret, beaming.

'Truce,' said Horrid Henry, scowling.

I'll get her for this, thought Horrid Henry. No one touches my flag and lives.

★

Horrid Henry watched and waited until it was dark and he heard the plinky-plonk sound of Moody Margaret practising her piano.

The coast was clear. Horrid Henry sneaked outside, jumped over the wall and darted inside the Secret Club Tent.

Swoop! He swept up the Secret Club pencils and secret code book.

Snatch! He snaffled the Secret Club stool.

Grab! He bagged the Secret Club biscuit tin.

Was that everything?

No!

Scoop! He snatched the Secret Club motto ('Down with boys').

Pounce! He pinched the Secret Club carpet.

Horrid Henry looked around. The Secret Club tent was bare.

Except for –

Henry considered. Should he?

Yes!

Whisk! The Secret Club tent collapsed. Henry gathered it into his arms with the rest of his spoils.

Huffing and puffing, gasping and panting, Horrid Henry staggered off over the wall, laden with the Secret Club. Raiding was hot, heavy work, but a pirate had to do his duty. Wouldn't all this booty look great decorating his fort?

A rug on the floor, an extra biscuit tin, a repainted motto – 'Down with girls' – yes, the Purple Hand Fort would have to be renamed the Purple Hand Palace.

Speaking of which, where was the Purple Hand Fort?

Horrid Henry looked about wildly for the Fort entrance.

It was gone.

He searched for the Purple Hand throne.

It was gone.

And the Purple Hand biscuit tin – GONE!

There was a rustling sound in the shadows. Horrid Henry turned and saw a strange sight.

There was the Purple Hand Fort leaning against the shed.

What?!

Suddenly the Fort started moving. Slowly, jerkily, the Fort wobbled across the lawn towards the wall on its four new stumpy legs.

Horrid Henry was livid. How dare

someone try to
nick his fort!
This was an
outrage. What
was the world
coming to,
when people
just sneaked into

your garden and made off with your
fort? Well, no way!

Horrid Henry let out a pirate roar.

'RAAAAAAAA!' roared Horrid
Henry.

'AHHHHHHH!' shrieked the Fort.
CRASH!

The Purple Hand Fort fell to the
ground. The raiders ran off, squabbling.

'I told you to hurry, you lazy lump!'

'You're the lazy lump!'

Victory!

Horrid Henry climbed to the top of

his fort and grabbed his banner. Waving it proudly, he chanted his victory chant: NAH NAH NE NAH NAH!

Henry's Holiday Howlers

What do sheep enjoy on a sunny day?

Having a baa-becue.

What do you call a
dog on a beach?

A hot dog.

Why did the elephant cross the road?

The chicken was on holiday.

How did the frog
cross the channel?

By hoppercraft.

Where do cows
go on holiday?

Moo Zealand.

Two cats were crossing the English Channel:
One, Two, Three and Un, Deux, Trois.
Which one won?

*One Two, Three because
Un, Deux, Trois Quatre Cinq!*

What do you get when
you cross an elephant
with a fish?

Swimming trunks.

HENRY'S MUM:
How much do you charge for a week's stay?

HOTEL MANAGER: *I don't know, no one's ever
stayed that long.*

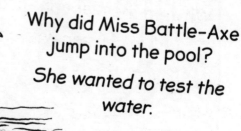

Why did Miss Battle-Axe
jump into the pool?

*She wanted to test the
water.*

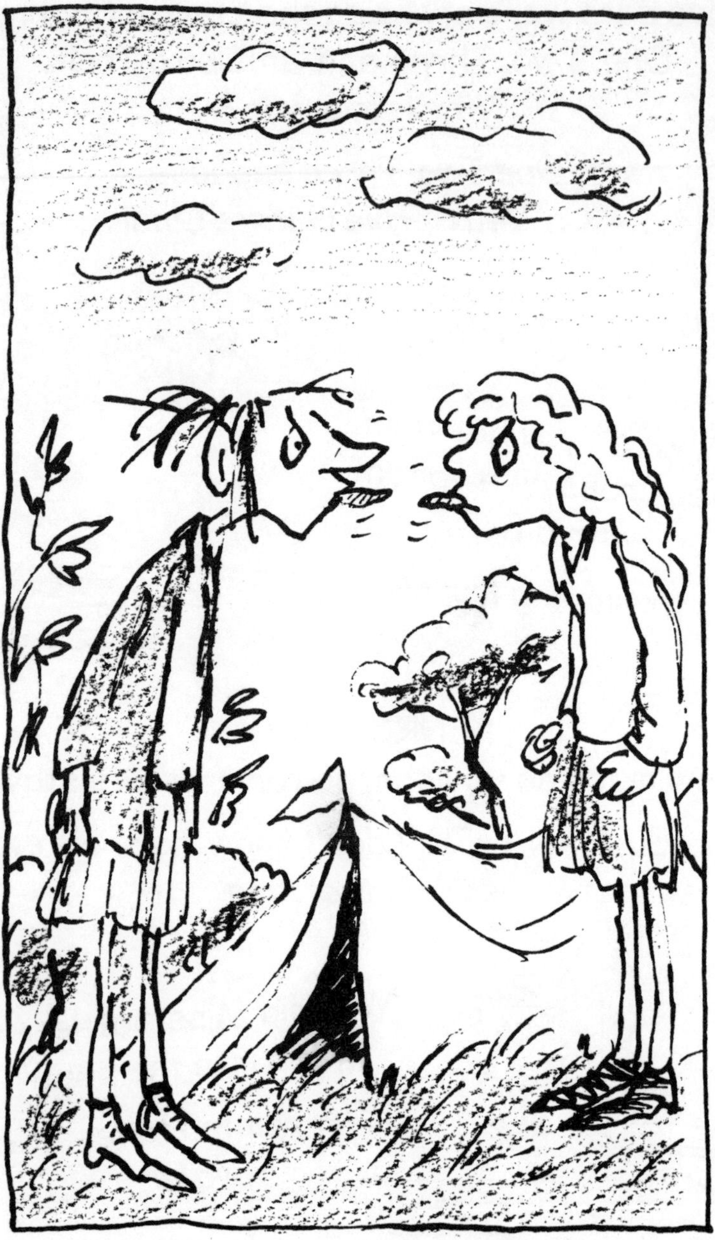

HORRID HENRY'S STINKBOMB

'I hate you, Margaret!' shrieked Sour Susan. She stumbled out of the Secret Club tent.

'I hate you too!' shrieked Moody Margaret.

Sour Susan stuck out her tongue. Moody Margaret stuck out hers back.

'I quit!' yelled Susan.

'You can't quit. You're fired!' yelled Margaret.

'You can't fire me. I quit!' said Susan.

123

'I fired you first,' said Margaret. 'And I'm changing the password!'

'Go ahead. See if I care. I don't want to be in the Secret Club any more!' said Susan sourly.

'Good! Because *we* don't want you.'

Moody Margaret flounced back inside the Secret Club tent. Sour Susan stalked off.

Free at last! Susan was sick and tired of her ex-best friend Bossyboots Margaret. Blaming *her* for the disastrous raid on the Purple Hand Fort when it was all Margaret's fault was bad enough. But then to ask stupid Linda to join the Secret Club without even telling her! Susan hated Linda even more than she hated Margaret. Linda hadn't invited Susan to her sleepover party. And she was a copycat. But Margaret didn't care. Today she'd made Linda chief spy.

Well, Susan had had enough. Margaret had been mean to her once too often.

Susan heard gales of laughter from inside the club tent. So they were laughing, were they? Laughing at her, no doubt? Well, she'd show them. She knew all about Margaret's Top Secret Plans. And she knew someone who would be very interested in that information.

★

'Halt! Password!'

'Smelly toads,' said Perfect Peter. He waited outside Henry's Purple Hand Fort.

'Wrong,' said Horrid Henry.

'What's the new one then?' said Perfect Peter.

'I'm not telling *you*,' said Henry. 'You're fired, remember?'

125

Perfect Peter did remember. He had hoped Henry had forgotten.

'Can't I join again, Henry?' asked Peter.

'No way!' said Horrid Henry.

'Please?' said Perfect Peter.

'No,' said Horrid Henry. 'Ralph's taken over your duties.'

Rude Ralph poked his head through the branches of Henry's lair.

'No babies allowed,' said Rude Ralph.

'We don't want you here, Peter,' said Horrid Henry. 'Get lost.'

Perfect Peter burst into tears.

'Crybaby!' jeered Horrid Henry.

'Crybaby!' jeered Rude Ralph.

That did it.

'Mum!' wailed Perfect Peter. He ran towards the house. 'Henry won't let me play and he called me a crybaby!'

'Stop being horrid, Henry!' shouted Mum.

Peter waited.

Mum didn't say anything else.

Perfect Peter started to wail louder.

'Muuum! Henry's being mean to me!'

'Leave Peter alone, Henry!' shouted Mum. She came out of the house. Her hands were covered in dough. 'Henry, if you don't stop—'

Mum looked around.

'Where's Henry?'

'In his fort,' snivelled Peter.

'I thought you said he was being mean to you,' said Mum.

'He was!' wailed Peter.

'Just keep away from him,' said Mum. She went back into the house.

Perfect Peter was outraged. Was that it? Why hadn't she punished Henry? Henry had been so horrid he deserved

to go to prison for a year. Two years. And just get a crust of bread a week. And brussels sprouts. Ha! That would serve Henry right.

But until Henry went to prison, how could Peter pay him back?

And then Peter knew exactly what he could do.

He checked carefully to see that no one was watching. Then he sneaked over the garden wall and headed for the Secret Club Tent.

★

'He isn't!' said Margaret.

'She wouldn't,' said Henry.

'He's planning to swap our lemonade for a Dungeon Drink?' said Margaret.

'Yes,' said Peter.

'She's planning to stinkbomb the Purple Hand Fort?' said Henry.

'Yes,' said Susan.

'How dare she?' said Henry.

'How dare he?' said Margaret. 'I'll easily put a stop to that. Linda!' she barked. 'Hide the lemonade!'

Linda yawned.

'Hide it yourself,' she said. 'I'm tired.'

Margaret glared at her, then hid the jug under a box.

'Ha ha! Won't Henry be shocked when he sneaks over and there are no drinks to spike!' gloated Margaret. 'Peter, you're a hero. I award you the Triple Star, the highest honour the Secret Club can bestow.'

'Ooh, thanks!' said Peter. It was nice being appreciated for a change.

'So from now on,' said Moody Margaret, 'you're working for me.'

'Okay,' said the traitor.

★

Horrid Henry rubbed his hands. This was fantastic! At last, he had a spy in the enemy's camp! He'd easily defend himself against that stupid stinkbomb. Margaret would only let it off when he was in the fort. His sentry would be on the lookout armed with a goo-shooter. When Margaret tried to sneak in with her stinkbomb — ker-pow!

'Hang on a sec,' said Horrid Henry, 'why should I trust you?'

131

'Because Margaret is mean and horrible and I hate her,' said Susan.

'So from now on,' said Horrid Henry, 'you're working for me.'

Susan wasn't sure she liked the sound of that. Then she remembered Margaret's mean cackle.

'Okay,' said the traitor.

★

Peter sneaked back into his garden and collided with someone.

'Ouch!' said Peter.

'Watch where you're going!' snapped Susan.

They glared at each other suspiciously.

'What were you doing at Margaret's?' said Susan.

'Nothing,' said Peter. 'What were you doing at my house?'

'Nothing,' said Susan.

Peter walked towards Henry's fort, whistling.

Susan walked towards Margaret's tent, whistling.

Well, if Susan was spying on Henry for Margaret, Peter certainly wasn't going to warn him. Serve Henry right.

Well, if Peter was spying on Margaret for Henry, Susan certainly wasn't going to warn her. Serve Margaret right.

★

Dungeon Drinks, eh?

Margaret liked that idea much better than her stinkbomb plot.

'I've changed my mind about the stinkbomb,' said Margaret. 'I'm going to swap his drinks for Dungeon Drink stinkers instead.'

'Good idea,' said Lazy Linda. 'Less work.'

★

Stinkbomb, eh?

Henry liked that much better than his dungeon drink plot. Why hadn't he thought of that himself?

'I've changed my mind about the Dungeon Drinks,' said Henry. 'I'm going to stinkbomb her instead.'

'Yeah,' said Rude Ralph. 'When?'

'Now,' said Horrid Henry. 'Come on, let's go to my room.'

Horrid Henry opened his Stinky
Stinkbomb kit. He'd bought it with
Grandma. Mum would never have let
him buy it. But because Grandma had
given him the money Mum couldn't do
anything about it. Ha ha ha.

Now, which pong would he pick?

He looked at the test tubes filled with
powder and read the gruesome labels.

Bad breath. Dog poo. Rotten eggs.
Smelly socks. Dead fish. Sewer stench.

'I'd go for dead fish,' said Ralph.

'That's the worst.'

Henry considered.

'How about we mix dead fish and rotten eggs?'

'Yeah,' said Rude Ralph.

Slowly, carefully, Horrid Henry measured out a teaspoon of Dead Fish powder, and a teaspoon of Rotten Egg powder, into the special pouch.

Slowly, carefully, Rude Ralph poured out 150 millilitres of secret stinkbomb liquid into the bottle and capped it tightly. All they had to do was to add

the powder to the bottle outside the
Secret Club and—run!

'Ready?' said Horrid Henry.

'Ready,' said Rude Ralph.

'Whatever you do,' said Horrid
Henry, 'don't spill it.'

★

'So you've come crawling back,' said
Moody Margaret. 'I knew you would.'

'No,' said Sour Susan. 'I just happened
to be passing.'

She looked around the Secret Club
Tent.

'Where's Linda?'

Margaret scowled. 'Gone.'

'Gone for today, or gone forever?' said
Susan.

'Forever,' said Margaret savagely. 'I
don't ever want to see that lazy lump
again.'

Margaret and Susan looked at each other.

Susan tapped her foot.

Margaret hummed.

'Well?' said Margaret.

'Well what?' said Susan.

'Are you rejoining the Secret Club as Chief Spy or aren't you?'

'I might,' said Susan. 'And I might not.'

'Suit yourself,' said Margaret. 'I'll call Gurinder and ask her to join instead.'

'Okay,' said Susan quickly. 'I'll join.'

Should she mention her visit to Henry? Better not. After all, what Margaret didn't know wouldn't hurt her.

'Now, about my stinkbomb plot,' began Margaret. 'I decided—'

Something shattered on the ground

inside the tent. A ghastly, gruesome, grisly stinky stench filled the air.

'AAAAARGGGGG!' screamed Margaret, gagging. 'It's a — STINKBOMB!'

'HELP!' shrieked Sour Susan. 'STINKBOMB! Help! Help!'

★

Victory! Horrid Henry and Rude Ralph ran back to the Purple Hand Fort and

139

rolled round the floor, laughing and
shrieking.

What a
triumph!
Margaret and
Susan screaming!
Margaret's mum
screaming!
Margaret's dad
screaming! And
the stink! Wow!
Horrid Henry
had never smelled
anything so awful in his life.

This called for a celebration.

Horrid Henry offered Ralph a fistful
of sweets and poured out two glasses of
Fizzywizz drinks.

'Cheers!' said Henry.

'Cheers!' said Ralph.

They drank.

'AAAAAARRGGGGGG!' choked Rude Ralph.

'Bleeeeeech!' yelped Horrid Henry, gagging and spitting. 'We've been—' cough!—'Dungeon-Drinked!'

And then Horrid Henry heard a horrible sound. Moody Margaret and Sour Susan were outside the Purple Hand Fort. Chanting a victory chant:

'NAH NAH NE NAH NAH!'

Henry's Holiday Howlers

What do horses suffer from in the summertime?

Neigh fever.

ANXIOUS ANDREW: Do these ships sink often?

CAPTAIN: *No, only once.*

Where do sheep go on holiday?

The Baa-hamas.

Why did the banana peel?

He forgot to put any sun cream on.

MISS BATTLE-AXE: What did you learn during the summer holidays, Henry?

HENRY: *That seven weeks isn't long enough to tidy my bedroom.*

VAIN VIOLET: I'm all red and blistered from sitting in the sun.

HENRY: Well, I guess you basked for it.

Why wasn't Sour Susan scared when she went swimming and saw a shark?

Because it was a man-eating shark.

HORRID HENRY'S SUMMER PUZZLE BOOK

HOLIDAY HOWLER

Follow the instructions then read the left over letters from left to right to find the punchline to Henry's howler.

Cross out: 5 Fs, 6 Js, 3 Ks, 7 Ms, 4 Ns, 7 Os, 4 Ps, 5 Qs, 4 Rs, 5 Xs, 6 Ys and 8 Zs

J	M	B	Q	P	E	O	Z	C
R	F	Y	A	X	N	U	K	Z
S	M	J	Z	F	Y	R	Z	E
M	Z	T	Q	O	H	Z	M	J
N	E	X	Z	P	Q	R	S	N
J	K	Y	E	O	X	A	Y	P
W	O	F	Q	M	R	F	O	M
P	Y	E	Z	X	J	K	Y	X
M	J	O	N	E	Q	F	O	D

QUESTION: Why did the crab blush?

ANSWER: __ __ __ __ __ __ __

__ __ __   __ __ __   __ __ __ __

Henry's Holiday Howlers

What do you call a man with
a seagull on his head?

Cliff.

Why is my child
so bright?

Because he is my son.

What do you call a cow
eating grass?

A lawnmoower.

Why can't cars play football?
They only have one boot.

Doctor, Doctor, I keep seeing insects spinning.
Don't worry. It's just a bug that's going round.

MY HOLIDAY HOWLERS

Can you write down five hilarious jokes
you've heard this summer?

1. _____

_____

_____

2. _____

_____

_____

3. _____

_____

_____

4. _____

_____

_____

5. _____

_____

_____

PIRATE PRANKS!

Colour in the picture opposite
and draw something horrid to fall on
Moody Margaret's head – and make
her even moodier.

What will you choose?

Goo?

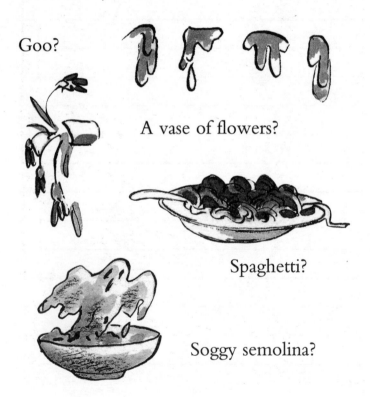

A vase of flowers?

Spaghetti?

Soggy semolina?

NOTE TO MOODY MARGARET

Can you work out what Horrid Henry's note says?

CLUB GRUB

Both the Purple Hand and the
Secret Club want the hidden store
of sweets. But which club wins?
Follow Henry and Margaret along
the rope to find out.

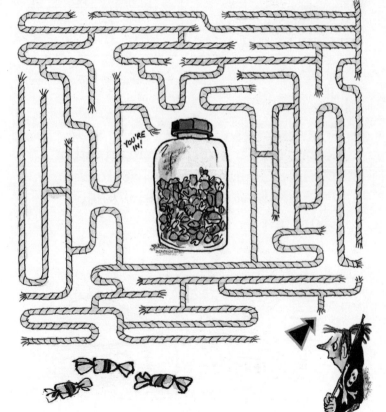

SWIMMING STARS

Can you work out who took part in which race, and which medals they won?

RACES: backstroke, crawl, butterfly
MEDALS: gold, silver and bronze

	RACE	POSITION
AEROBIC AL		
GREEDY GRAHAM		
MOODY MARGARET		

Clues

1. Moody Margaret didn't do as well in her race as Greedy Graham did in his
2. Greedy Graham did the backstroke
3. The person who did the butterfly came first

FOOTBALL FUN

Henry is using all his skills – elbowing,
barging, pushing and shoving – to win the
game. See if you can spot where the ball
should be on these three pictures.
Draw an X to mark the spot.

FAMILY MIX-UP

Do you know the names of Horrid Henry's family? Can you un-muddle the words below and complete their names?

Write your answers here:

1. PRISSY **YLOPL** _ _ _ _ _
2. RICH AUNT **BYUR** _ _ _ _
3. PIMPLY **UPAL** _ _ _ _
4. GREAT-AUNT **AETRG** _ _ _ _ _
5. VOMITING **RVAE** _ _ _ _
6. STUCK-UP **EETVS** _ _ _ _ _

HORRID HENRY NAMES

Can you think up your own Horrid Henry names for your family and friends? Remember to start both words with the same letter for every name.

_____

_____

_____

_____

_____

_____

_____

_____

_____

_____

_____

H WORDS

Can you fit all the H words below
into the criss-cross puzzle?
Start with the longest word.

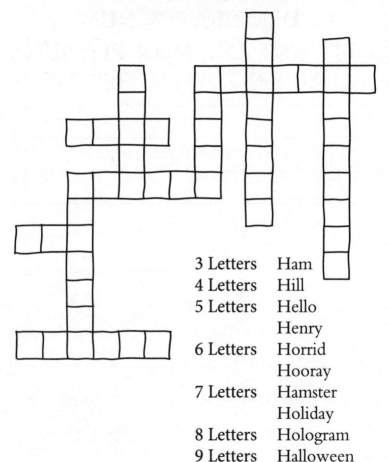

3 Letters	Ham
4 Letters	Hill
5 Letters	Hello
	Henry
6 Letters	Horrid
	Hooray
7 Letters	Hamster
	Holiday
8 Letters	Hologram
9 Letters	Halloween

SPLIT WORDS

Here are eight six-letter words, but they have all been split in half. Can you solve the clues and put the pairs together?

DER NIC PER NUM
BIT NUT LET MON PEA JUM
RAB SPI KEY PIG BER PIC

A baby pig	PIG	LET
A meal eaten outside, packed in a hamper		
Something you wear when it's cold		
An animal with long ears and a fluffy tail		
A cheeky animal with a long tail		
It can be bought salted or in its shell		
100 is one, and so is 7		
A creepy crawly that spins a web		

MUSEUM MAZE

CLITTER-CLATTER! Horrid Henry has
wrecked the skeleton in the Town Museum,
and the guards are after him. Can you help
Horrid Henry find his way out?

MUMMY MUDDLE

Horrid Henry is a menace with the Mummy Kit. Can you untangle the loo roll trail, and discover who he has wrapped up today?

FLUFFY

MUM

161

PETER

CODE LETTERS

Horrid Henry has written a note to Perfect Peter. He's used a secret code so that his mum and dad won't read it and stop him watching TV. Can you break the code and read the note?

CLUE: If A = Z and Z = A, can you work out all the letters in between?

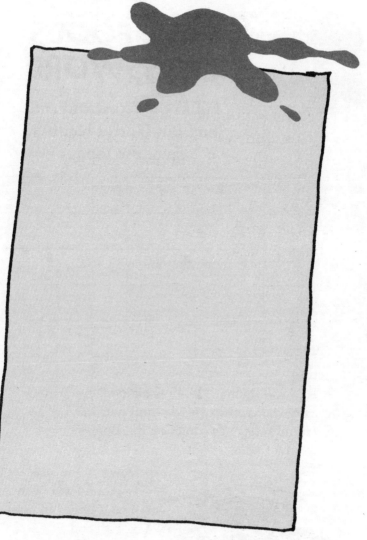

Now use Horrid Henry's code to write
your own note to Perfect Peter.

FAVE FOODS CROSSWORD

Fill in the crossword and find out Horrid Henry's favourite foods.

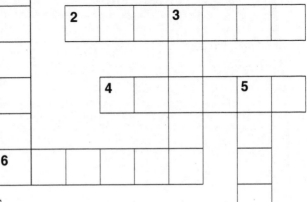

Across

2 Red and squirty – looks like blood!

4 Salty and crunchy. Made from potatoes.

6 Horrid Henry's favourites are Big Boppers and Dirt Balls.

Down

1 Round and beefy, and served in buns.

3 Fish and _ _ _ _ _!

5 Big and round, with cheese and tomato on top.

164

HORRIBLY HEALTHY FOOD

Henry's mum is planning a horribly healthy menu for Horrid Henry's party. To find out the menu fill in the answers on the dotted lines below.

1. Horrid Henry hates this fruit.
   It's green or red, with a core.
   _ _ _ _ _ JUICE

2. These fruits are green or black
   and come in bunches.

   _ _ _ _ _ _

3. A long salad vegetable
   with dark green skin.
   _ _ _ _ _ _ _ _ SANDWICHES

4. An orange vegetable.
   _ _ _ _ _ _ CAKE

5. A pale green salad vegetable,
   eaten with dips.
   _ _ _ _ _ _ STICKS

WHAT'S FOR TEA?

Cross out all the letters that appear more than once on Horrid Henry's plate. Then rearrange the letters that are left to find out why he looks so angry.

Write your answer here: __ __ __ __

CRAZY COOKS

Solve the clues below and fill in the
missing words – they are all things you
might find in your kitchen. Then read
down the dark column to reveal
something horrible cooked up by
Horrid Henry and Moody Margaret.

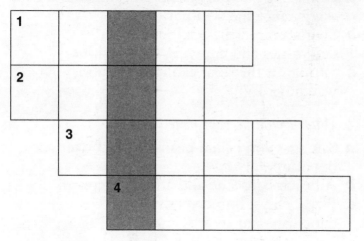

1. Add a teaspoon of this
   to sweeten your tea
2. This comes from cows
3. This is made by bees
4. This comes in different shapes,
   like spaghetti and macaroni

HAPPY HOLiDAYS

Henry's idea of a good holiday just isn't the same as his mum and dad's. What sort of holiday would suit you? Imagine your dream holiday, and answer these questions.

1. *What do you dream of doing on holiday?*

a Going for good long walks in the countryside – whatever the weather.

b Swimming in the sea, building sandcastles and enjoying the sunshine.

c Sitting on the sofa, eating crisps and watching TV.

2. *What would be your perfect meal?*

a Sausages and baked beans cooked over an open fire.

b A beach barbecue and a big ice-cream.

c Pizza, chips, burgers, crisps, chocolate and sweets.

3. *What would you be wearing on your dream holiday?*

a Walking boots, thick socks, waterproof trousers, woolly jumper and an anorak.

b Swimming trunks or a bikini.

c Pyjamas – it's a holiday!

4. *What would you bring back with you?*

a Muddy boots and soggy wet clothes.
b A collection of pebbles and shells.
c A collection of sweet wrappers and crisp packets.

5. *What are your top three tips for a dream holiday?*

a Fresh air, cold showers and quiet.
b Sun, sea and sand.
c Comfy beds, hot baths and a giant TV with fifty-seven channels.

ANSWERS

Mostly a's:
Unlike Henry, you like a challenge, and your ideal holiday is a camping trip without any home comforts.

Mostly b's: A traditional seaside holiday is your idea of bliss. So pack up your swimming gear, and your bucket and spade, and enjoy a fun-filled beach break.

Mostly c's: Just like Horrid Henry, your idea of a perfect holiday would be to spend every day grossing out on pizza, chips, crisps and sweets and watching all your favourite TV programmes.

CAMPSITE MAZE

Horrid Henry and his family travel on the ferry to France, and then drive to the campsite. But which campsite will they arrive at – Horrid Henry's favourite, Lazy Life, or Perfect Peter's choice?

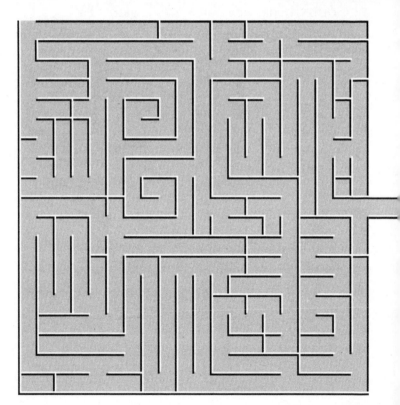

MY DREAM HOLiDAY

Horrid Henry dreams of going on holiday
to Lazy Life Campsite where there is
swimming, music and TV.
Draw a picture of your dream holiday here.

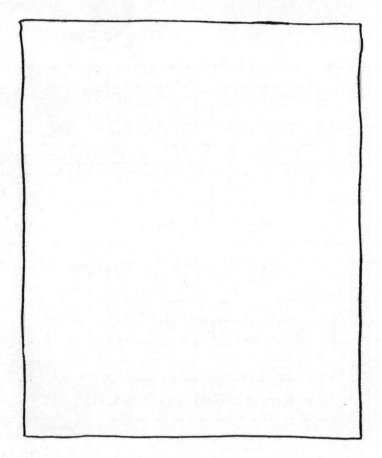

HOLIDAY HIGHLIGHTS

Horrid Henry's family, friends, and enemies have special holiday highlights. Untangle the names and work out who enjoyed what.

1. Day out at a theme park **EAATGRMR**

   Answer: __ __ __ __ __ __ __

2. Watching a football match **SMSI ELBTTA-XEA**

   Answer: __ __ __ __   __ __ __ __ __ __ - __ __ __

3. Swimming with dolphins **GGSYO DSI**

   Answer: __ __ __ __ __ __ __ __

4. Long lie-ins every day **DNLIA**

   Answer: __ __ __ __ __

5. Trip to an ice cream factory **MGAAHR**

   Answer: __ __ __ __ __ __

6. Going on a nature trail **RPTEE**

   Answer: __ __ __ __ __

7. Attending the Summer School for Clever Kids **NBRAI** and **EALCR**

   Answer: __ __ __ __ __ and

__ __ __ __ 173

ARE YOU A HORRID HENRY OR A PERFECT PETER?

Are you like Horrid Henry –
or more like Perfect Peter?

1. *What do you do with your pocket money?*

a Spend it all on sweets and comics.
b Save it up to buy something special.

2. *Is your bedroom…*

a A smelly mess covered in sweet wrappers
and old comics?
b Always neat and clean?

3. *When your parents have guests round
to the house, do you…*

a Try to spoil their evening by being on
your worst behaviour?
b Help hand round nibbles and nod
politely at everything they say?

4. *If you have nits…*

a Do you pass them on to as many people as possible?

b You never get nits!

5. *If the queen visited your school, would you…*

a Ask her how many TVs she has?

b Bow and say hello. You've been practising for weeks.

6. *If your parents asked you to vacuum the living room, would you…*

a Leave the vacuum on while you watch TV?

b Get to it right away? You need some extra pocket money for that new science book.

Mostly a's: You are a Horrid Henry! You're messy, rude, lazy and – horrid!

Mostly b's: You are a Perfect Peter. You're neat and nice, polite and – perfect!

WHAT'S IN THE BAG?

Horrid Henry's holiday bag is full of comics
and sweets, but can you guess what
Perfect Peter has in his?

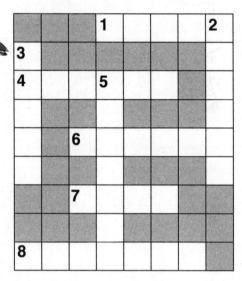

Across

1. Use this to draw a straight line.
4. You can write or draw with this.
6. Square and white – for blowing your nose.
7. You can borrow this from a library.
8. If you cut your knee, use one of these.

Down

2. You can use this if you make a mistake.
3. Something healthy to eat on the journey.
5. These can add colour to your work.

PERFECT PETER'S PICTURES

Henry has been doodling on Perfect Peter's school photos. Can you spot the pairs?

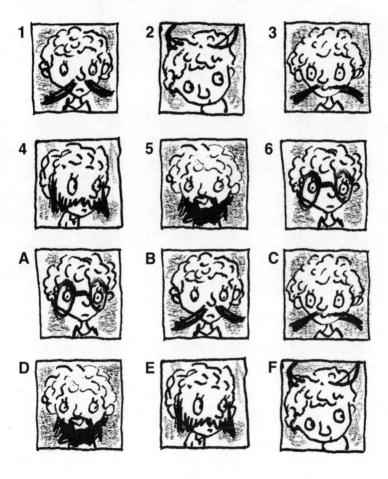

BiRTHDAY PRESENTS

Horrid Henry's birthday was in February,
but he's still mad about the presents he got.
Can you find all his unwanted presents
listed below in the wordsearch?

BOOK   **SCRABBLE**   **PANTS**
PENS   **GLOBE**   **VEST**
CARDIGAN **SOAP**   **PAPER**

P	P	T	W	H	O	O	E	C
A	A	S	P	E	E	L	A	R
O	N	E	C	U	B	R	S	E
S	T	V	H	B	D	I	O	P
N	S	V	A	I	N	M	J	A
Q	O	R	G	S	N	E	P	P
F	C	A	X	G	L	O	B	E
S	N	K	O	O	B	Z	X	H
R	B	T	S	X	F	X	M	W

Now find the first 14 left over letters and
see if you can read the hidden message.
It reveals the present that Horrid Henry
really wanted. Write your answer here:

_ _ _ _ _ _ _ / _ _ _ _ _ _ _

Now colour in this picture of Horrid Henry
dreaming of his favourite toys to take
on holiday.

SPORTS DAY

Horrid Henry, Perfect Peter and Moody Margaret each took part in a different race. One of them came 1st, one of them came 2nd and one of them came 3rd. From the clues, work out who competed in which race, and what their position was.

RACES: skipping, sack, egg and spoon

	RACE	POSITION
HORRID HENRY		
PERFECT PETER		
MOODY MARGARET		

Clues

1. Horrid Henry didn't do as well in his race as Moody Margaret did in hers.
2. Moody Margaret did the skipping race.
3. The person who did the egg and spoon race came first.

SPORT SEARCH

Can you find all the sports listed below
in the wordsearch?

**BADMINTON GOLF
ROUNDERS
HOCKEY NETBALL
TENNIS RUGBY
CRICKET FOOTBALL**

B	T	D	Q	Z	X	E	R	F
P	A	E	D	T	B	O	H	O
F	T	D	N	J	U	X	O	O
C	L	E	M	N	Q	Y	C	T
E	I	O	D	I	I	B	K	B
F	T	E	G	P	N	S	E	A
C	R	I	C	K	E	T	Y	L
S	J	Y	B	G	U	R	O	L
L	L	A	B	T	E	N	X	N

181

HORRiD HENRY'S SPORTS DAY

Write your own Horrid Henry story
about the horrid tricks Henry gets up to
at his school sports day.

_____

_____

_____

_____

_____

_____

_____

_____

_____

_____

_____

_____

Read all about Horrid Henry's Sports Day
in *Horrid Henry Gets Rich Quick*

TRiCKY TRiANGLES

Miss Battle-Axe has given her class two
puzzles to solve over the holidays.
Can you do them too?

In the first puzzle, move the numbers on to
the rings, so that the total of the numbers
on all three sides of the triangle equals 9.

Numbers
1
2
3
4
5
6

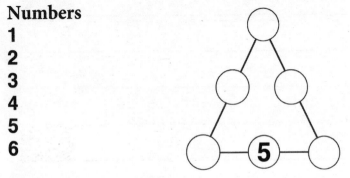

Why not try another?
This time, all the sides have to equal 10.

Numbers
1
2
3
4
5
6

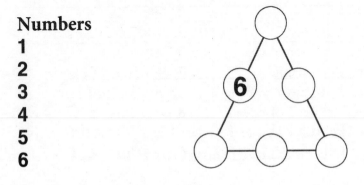

CROSS NUMBERS

Here's a crossword with a difference – it's all numbers! Henry is horrified! So give him a hand with his maths and help him fill it in.

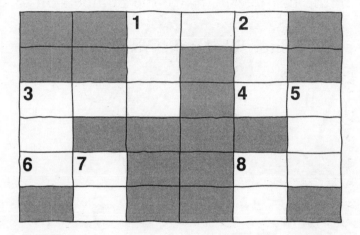

Across

1. Number of days in a year
3. 12 x 12
4. Number of days in a fortnight
6. Add 22 to 8 across
8. Number of days in February in a leap year

Down

1. 1 across plus 8 across
2. 499 + 2
3. Add 21 to 3 across
5. 501 – 2
7. Number of players in a football team
8. 7 down x 2

JOIN THE NITS

Moody Margaret's head is crawling with nits. Can you join up the nits and reveal who's holding the scary-looking nit comb?

PET PUZZLE

Can you find the following pets
in the wordsearch below?

GOLDFISH   HORSE

PARROT   TORTOISE

GUINEA PIG   KITTEN

PUPPY   HAMSTER

MOUSE   RABBIT

E	S	I	O	T	R	O	T	G
G	F	H	A	H	Y	N	I	K
R	O	G	A	P	O	P	J	I
A	H	L	P	M	A	R	P	T
B	E	U	D	E	S	A	S	T
B	P	S	N	F	R	T	S	E
I	Y	I	U	R	I	H	E	N
T	U	X	O	O	B	S	O	R
G	N	T	Z	Q	M	S	H	X

CLASSMATE CROSSWORD

Can you fill in the crossword
with the names of some of
Horrid Henry's classmates?

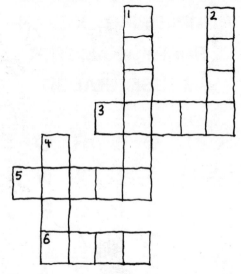

Across

3. _ _ _ _ _ **BERT** (Biggest boy in the class)
5. _ _ _ _ _ **JOSH** (Always happy)
6. _ _ _ _ **RALPH** (Never says please or thank you!)

Down

1. _ _ _ _ _ _ **GRAHAM** (Eats lots of sweets)
2. _ _ _ _ **LINDA** (Does as little as possible)
4. _ _ _ _ **SUSAN** (Like a lemon!)

WEEPY WILLIAM'S DISAPPOINTING DISGUISE

These six pictures of Weepy William
on Hallowe'en all look the same.
Can you spot the odd one out?

1  **2**  **3**

4 **5**  **6**

SANDWICHES

Put one letter in the dark column that will finish the first word and begin the second word. For example, S could be placed between BU and MILE to make BUS and SMILE.

BU	S	MILE
CA		RAIN
YET		GLOO
FU		APPY
BOO		ITE
CLU		ALL
YOY		VAL
PLU		USIC
WE		OOT

When you've finished, the middle column spells out something that will make Horrid Henry smile!

Answer: __ __ __ __ __ __ __ __ __

PiCTURE PAIRS

Perfect Peter does a lovely picture of their ferry to France, until Henry doodles on it. There are three pairs of pictures below – can you find them?

A

B

D

C

E

F

Answer:

The three pairs are: _____ _____ _____

CAR GAMES

Look out of the car window and see if you
can spot something beginning with every
letter of Horrid Henry's name.
Write your answers here when you do.

H _____

O _____

R _____

R _____

I _____

D _____

H _____

E _____

N _____

R _____

Y _____

Now see if you can spot all of the things on Horrid Henry's list. Tick them off when you see them.

☐ 6 red cars

☐ 4 blue cars

☐ A motorbike

☐ A dog in the back of a car

☐ Somewhere that sells burgers

☐ A registration plate with an H in it

☐ A field of sheep

TOP SECRET JOKES

Some of Horrid Henry's jokes
are so rude, he has to write the
answers in his top secret code.
Can you understand what
Henry has written?

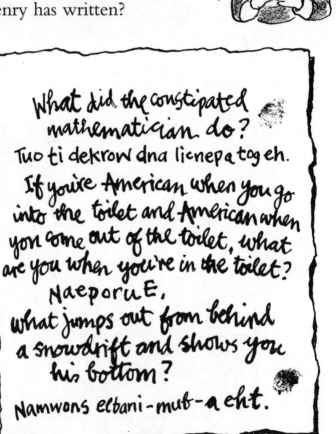

What did the constipated
mathematician do?

Tuo ti dekrow dna licnepa tog eh.

If you're American when you go
into the toilet and American when
you come out of the toilet, what
are you when you're in the toilet?

NaeporuE.

what jumps out from behind
a snowdrift and shows you
his bottom?

Namwons elbani-mub-a eht.

194

HENRY'S HORRIBLY HARD WORDSEARCH

Can you find the list of horribly hard words below in the wordsearch?

BATTLEAXE   HIEROGLYPHS

CANNIBALS   LAZORZAP

DIARRHOEA

TERMINATOR

FANGMANGLER

TRAPEZIUM

F	S	A	T	N	V	B	N	L	B	J
A	H	K	E	D	C	P	G	A	D	U
N	P	X	R	O	L	Q	T	Z	G	R
G	Y	S	M	G	H	T	I	O	U	O
M	L	H	I	S	L	R	K	R	P	S
A	G	A	N	E	D	C	R	Z	N	U
N	O	C	A	N	N	I	B	A	L	S
G	R	X	T	J	W	F	G	P	I	Z
L	E	G	O	I	L	S	E	U	M	D
E	I	L	R	R	I	M	H	R	C	I
R	H	M	U	I	Z	E	P	A	R	T

WHAT'S IN THE BOX?

Cross out all the letters that appear more than three times on Horrid Henry's box. Then rearrange the five letters that are left to find out what's inside.

Write your answer here: _ _ _ _ _ KIT

JOIN THE DOTS

"It's as long as my leg," said Moody Margaret. Join the dots to find out what Moody Margaret is talking about, and why Horrid Henry is looking so scared.

Write your answer here: _ _ _ _ _ _

CODE CRACKING

When Greasy Greta,
the demon dinner lady,
starts pinching all
the tasty treats from
Horrid Henry's
lunch, it's time
for revenge.

Crack the code
and discover his plan.

G D   L Z J D R   G N S

B G H K K H   A H R B T H S R

CODE CRACKING CLUE:
Replace every letter here with the next
letter from the alphabet.

SEASiDE SUDOKUS

Can you solve these seaside sudokus?
Every coloured box must contain one shell,
one starfish, one sun and one ice cream.

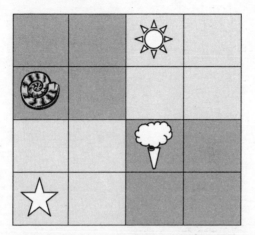

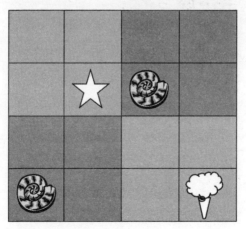

Goodbye!

ANSWERS

p147
BECAUSE THE SEA WEED

p.152
Margaret, you Worm.
Watch out!
The Purple Hand is on the attack.
We will steal your biscuits and your dagger.
NAH NAH NEE NAH NAH.
Horrid Henry.

p153

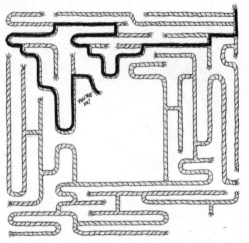

The Purple Hand Club wins.

p.154

	RACE	POSITION
AEROBIC AL	BUTTERFLY	GOLD
GREEDY GRAHAM	BACKSTROKE	SILVER
MOODY MARGARET	CRAWL	BRONZE

p.155

p.156
1. Prissy Polly, 2. Rich Aunt Ruby, 3. Pimply Paul
4. Great-Aunt Greta, 5. Vomiting Vera, 6. Stuck-Up Steve

p.158

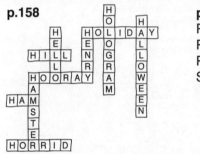

p.159
PIC-NIC, JUM-PER,
RAB-BIT, MON-KEY
PEA-NUT, NUM-BER,
SPI-DER

p.160

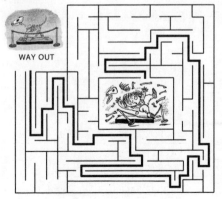

p.161
Horrid Henry has wrapped up Fluffy today

p.162
PETER IS SMELLY

p.164
1 down – Burgers
2 across - Ketchup
3 down – Chips
4 across - Crisps
5 down - Pizza
6 across - Sweets

p.165
APPLE juice, GRAPES,
CUCUMBER sandwiches
CARROT cake, CELERY
sticks

p.166
Horrid Henry doesn't like his PEAS

p.167

S	U	G	A	R	
M	I	L	K		
	H	O	N	E	Y
		P	A	S	T	A

Horrid Henry and Moody Margaret cooked up GLOP.

p.170-171

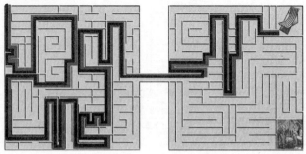

204

p.173

1. MARGARET, 2. MISS BATTLE-AXE, 3. SOGGY SID
4. LINDA, 5. GRAHAM, 6. PETER, 7. BRIAN and CLARE

p.176

1 across - Ruler, 2 down - Rubber,
3 down - Apple, 4 across - Pencil,
5 down - Crayons, 6 across - Hankie,
7 across - Book, 8 across - Plaster

p.177

1-B, 2-F, 3-C, 4-E,
5-D, 6-A

p.178

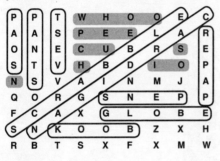

The hidden message is:
WHOOPEE CUSHION

p.180

	RACE	POSITION
HORRID HENRY	SACK	3RD
PERFECT PETER	EGG AND SPOON	1ST
MOODY MARGARET	SKIPPING	2ND

p.181

p.184

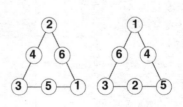

205

p185

		3	6	5	
		9		0	
1	4	4		1	4
6					9
5	1			2	9
	1			2	

p.186

Nitty Nora, the nit nurse

p.187

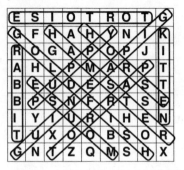

p.188

1 down - Greedy, 2 down - Lazy, 3 across - Beefy
4 down - Sour, 5 across - Jolly, 6 across – Rude

p.189

The odd one out is number 4. Weepy William's ear is missing

p.190

STINKBOMB

p.191

The pairs are A and C, D and F, B and E

p.194

Read backwards

p.195

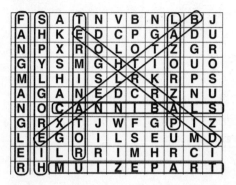

p.196
MUMMY KIT

p.197
It's a NEEDLE

p.198
HE MAKES HOT CHILLI BISCUITS

p.199

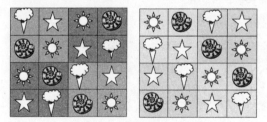

HORRID HENRY BOOKS

Storybooks

Horrid Henry
Horrid Henry and the Secret Club
Horrid Henry Tricks the Tooth Fairy
Horrid Henry's Nits
Horrid Henry Gets Rich Quick
Horrid Henry's Haunted House
Horrid Henry and the Mummy's Curse
Horrid Henry's Revenge
Horrid Henry and the Bogey Babysitter
Horrid Henry's Stinkbomb
Horrid Henry's Underpants
Horrid Henry Meets the Queen

Early Readers

Don't be Horrid Henry
Horrid Henry's Birthday Party
Horrid Henry's Holiday
Horrid Henry's Underpants
Horrid Henry Gets Rich Quick
Horrid Henry and the Football Fiend
Horrid Henry's Nits
Horrid Henry and Moody Margaret
Horrid Henry's Thank You Letter
Horrid Henry Car Journey
Moody Margaret's School
Horrid Henry's Tricks and Treats
Horrid Henry's Rainy Day
Horrid Henry's Author Visit
Horrid Henry Meets the Queen

Joke Books

Horrid Henry's Joke Book
Horrid Henry's Jolly Joke Book
Horrid Henry's Mighty Joke Book
Horrid Henry versus Moody Margaret
Horrid Henry's Hilariously Horrid Joke Book
Horrid Henry's Purple Hand Gang Joke Book
Horrid Henry's All Time Favourite Joke Book
Horrid Henry's Jumbo Joke Book

Activity Books

Horrid Henry's Brainbusters
Horrid Henry's Headscratchers
Horrid Henry's Mindbenders
Horrid Henry's Colouring Book
Horrid Henry's Puzzle Book
Horrid Henry's Sticker Book
Horrid Henry Runs Riot
Horrid Henry's Classroom Chaos
Horrid Henry's Holiday Havoc
Horrid Henry's Wicked Wordsearches
Horrid Henry's Mad Mazes
Horrid Henry's Crazy Crosswords
Horrid Henry's Gold Medal Games

Fact Books

Horrid Henry's Ghosts
Horrid Henry's Dinosaurs
Horrid Henry's Sports
Horrid Henry's Food
Horrid Henry's King and Queens
Horrid Henry's Bugs
Horrid Henry's Animals
Horrid Henry's Ghosts
Horrid Henry's Crazy Creatures

WHERE'S HORRID HENRY

Featuring 32 pages of fiendish things to spot, join Henry and his friends (and evilest enemies!) on their awesome adventures – from birthday parties and camping trips to hiding out at a spooky haunted house. With a challenging checklist of things to find, this is Henry's most horrid challenge yet!

The question is, where's Horrid Henry?

HORRiD HENRY'S GOLD MEDAL GAMES

On your marks, get set . . .
go for gold with Horrid Henry!

Go for gold with this utterly wicked and
totally brilliant activity book.
Full of gruesome games, puzzles and
activities, plus a range of scenes to colour,
Henry goes up against his nemesis,
Moody Margaret – and he's playing to win!

But will you be a wicked winner?

HORRID HENRY'S CANNIBAL CURSE

The final collection of four brand new utterly horrid stories in which Horrid Henry triumphantly reveals his guide to perfect parents, reads an interesting book about a really naughty girl, and conjures up the cannibal's curse to deal with his enemies and small, annoying brother.

Visit Horrid Henry's website at
www.horridhenry.co.uk for competitions,
games, downloads and a monthly newsletter